Poppy Cat

For our very own
paw-printing,
paper-tearing,
tea-drinking
Poppy Cat x

Scholastic Canada Ltd.
604 King Street West, Toronto, Ontario M5V 1E1, Canada

Scholastic Inc.
557 Broadway, New York, NY 10012, USA

Scholastic Australia Pty Limited
PO Box 579, Gosford, NSW 2250, Australia

Scholastic New Zealand Limited
Private Bag 94407, Botany, Manukau 2163, New Zealand

Scholastic Children's Books
Euston House, 24 Eversholt Street, London NW1 1DB, UK

www.scholastic.ca

Library and Archives Canada Cataloguing in Publication
Acton, Sara, author, illustrator
Poppy cat / Sarah Acton.

Orginally published: Lindfield, NSW : Scholastic Australia, 2014.
ISBN 978-1-4431-3933-5 (bound)

I. Title.

PZ10.3.A33Po 2015   j823'.92   C2014-907072-1

First published by Scholastic Australia in 2014.
This edition published by Scholastic Canada Ltd. in 2015.

6 5 4 3 2 1   Printed in Malaysia 108   15 16 17 18 19

Poppy Cat

Sara Acton

Scholastic Canada Ltd.
Toronto New York London Auckland Sydney
Mexico City New Delhi Hong Kong Buenos Aires

Poppy Cat is a copy cat.

She follows me wherever I go.

She does whatever I do.

Sometimes, when I am getting dressed,
I have problems putting my head
through the right hole.

So does Poppy.

Sometimes, when I am trying to do up
my shoelaces

I get all tangled up.

So does Poppy.

I like to do things all by myself.

Sometimes I make a mess.

So does Poppy.

When the sun is shining
Poppy likes to explore.

She is very good at

hiding,

creeping

and

pouncing.

And when it rains Poppy likes to watch
the raindrops race down the window pane
and chase them with her paw.

Poppy is usually a good cat.

But sometimes she is mischievous . . .

And sometimes she wants to be all by herself.

But at the end of the day, when I curl up on the sofa,
Poppy Cat curls up with me ...

and purrs.